DATE	ISSUED TO
NOV 2 9 2004	
MAR 1 2 2005	
APR 0 5 2005	
APR 2 9 2005	
MAY 1 8 2005	
OCT 1 2 2005	

© DEMCO 32-2125

Barbie

Hi! My name is Barbie. I have some rules to live by—rules that help me be the best person I can be. I call them . . .

Barbie Rules! #3

No Teasing Allowed!

By Louise Gikow • Illustrations by Karen Wolcott
Cover photography by Tom Wolfson, Susan Kurtz, Tim Geisen,
Sawako Iizuka, Scott Meskill, Lisa Collins, and Judy Tsuno

 A GOLDEN BOOK • NEW YORK

BARBIE and associated trademarks are owned by and used under license from Mattel, Inc.
Copyright © 2003 Mattel, Inc. All Rights Reserved.
Published in the United States by Golden Books, an imprint of Random House Children's Books, a division of
Random House, Inc., New York, and simultaneously in Canada by Random House of Canada Limited, Toronto.
No part of this book may be reproduced or copied in any form without written permission from the copyright
owner. Golden Books, A Golden Book, and the G colophon are registered trademarks of Random House, Inc.
Library of Congress Control Number: 2002113658   ISBN: 0-307-10357-9
www.goldenbooks.com   Printed in the United States of America   10 9 8 7 6 5 4 3 2 1

"Poor Amanda!" Stacie sighed, flopping down on her bed after school.

"Amanda? Who's Amanda?" I asked.

"She's this new girl," Stacie explained. "She lives near here, and we walk home together every day."

"So what's the matter with Amanda?" I asked.

"Melinda and Holly are giving her a really hard time," Stacie explained.

Uh-oh, I thought. I'd heard a lot about Melinda and Holly. They were very popular, and they were always teasing people.

"The first day Amanda came to school, she was dressed a little different," Stacie explained. "She didn't wear the same clothes that everyone wears at our school.

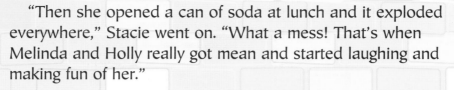

"Then she opened a can of soda at lunch and it exploded everywhere," Stacie went on. "What a mess! That's when Melinda and Holly really got mean and started laughing and making fun of her."

"So what are you going to do about it?" I asked Stacie.

"Me? What can I do?" Stacie said.

"Why don't you invite Amanda over to do homework?" I suggested gently. "After all, she lives nearby . . . and she's probably feeling pretty lonely, being new and all."

"Good idea!" Stacie said. "I'll ask her."

Amanda came over to our house a little later. She was very sweet, and I liked her right away. Stacie liked her, too. They were having a lot of fun together.

The next day, though, was no fun at all.

When Stacie and Amanda got to school, Melinda and Holly were outside.

"Look at that," Melinda said. "Stacie and the new girl. Boy, you'd think Stacie would have better taste. . . ."

Holly laughed. "Well, if Stacie wants to hang out with Amanda, that's her problem."

After Melinda and Holly went inside, Amanda turned to Stacie.

"You don't have to hang out with me if you don't want to," Amanda said sadly.

Stacie shook her head. "I *do* want to," she said. "You're my friend. Melinda and Holly are wrong to tease you. Don't let them bother you."

But over the next few weeks, it seemed that no matter where Amanda and Stacie went, Melinda and Holly were there, too.

Melinda and Holly whispered and giggled and pointed at Amanda and Stacie. They broke one of my major rules— no teasing allowed.

Making fun of someone is, well . . . just plain wrong. One of the worst things a person can do is tease other people and make them feel bad about themselves.

Stacie and Amanda thought and thought about what they could do to stop Melinda and Holly's teasing. They even asked me about it.

"I know it's hard, but you just have to ignore people who tease," I said. "Hopefully, Melinda and Holly will realize it's not nice to tease, or to be teased."

"Okay, we'll try," Amanda and Stacie said.

The next day, Amanda and Stacie were watching some guys play basketball. When the ball bounced over to the girls, Amanda picked it up with one hand and tossed it toward the basket without even looking—and it went in!

"How'd you do *that*?" Stacie asked.

"I have four older brothers," Amanda said with a grin. "They taught me how to play basketball."

"You should join the Eagles basketball team in gym class," Stacie said.

"But Melinda and Holly are on the team," Amanda said. "I don't know. . . ."

"Don't let them stop you," Stacie said. "You're good!"

"All right," Amanda said with a smile.

So Amanda joined the team, but Melinda and Holly were still mean. They didn't talk to her, they hogged the ball, and they acted as if she weren't there.

But they couldn't ignore Amanda's skill on the court.
The team was on its way to becoming school champions!

On the day of the big game, the Eagles and the Blue Jays were tied at 50 to 50. Then, with only minutes to go, Melinda tried to block a Blue Jays shot at the basket. But she accidentally tipped the ball in and gave two points to the Blue Jays!

Melinda's teammates gave her a hard time for making a basket for the wrong team.

Amanda heard all the teasing and felt sorry for Melinda. She knew what it felt like to be teased.

Amanda went over to Melinda and said shyly, "Don't feel bad. Everyone makes mistakes."

"Thanks," Melinda said slowly. "I can't believe you're being nice to me, especially after the way I've treated you. I'm sorry I teased you."

Holly overheard Melinda's conversation with Amanda, and she apologized for her behavior, too.

"Friends?" Melinda and Holly asked.

"Friends!" Amanda said.

The new friends worked together during the last minutes of the game—and the Eagles won!

Stacie and I were very proud of Amanda. She could have teased Melinda . . . but she didn't. And in my book, that made her a star both on and off the court.